For my children and their friends,
and in memory of my grandmother.

VIKING
Published by the Penguin Group
Viking Penguin, a division of Penguin Books USA Inc.,
375 Hudson Street, New York, New York 10014, U.S.A.
Penguin Books Ltd, 27 Wrights Lane, London W8 5TZ, England
Penguin Books Australia Ltd, Ringwood, Victoria, Australia
Penguin Books Canada Ltd, 2801 John Street, Markham, Ontario, Canada L3R 1B4
Penguin Books (N.Z.) Ltd, 182-190 Wairau Road, Auckland 10, New Zealand
Penguin Books Ltd, Registered Offices: Harmondsworth, Middlesex, England

First published in Great Britain by Heinemann Young Books 1990

First American edition published 1990

10   9   8   7   6   5   4   3   2   1

Original text copyright © Juliet Harmer 1990
Illustrations copyright © Juliet Harmer 1990
Text adapted for this edition by Viking Penguin

Library of Congress catalog number: 89-52219
ISBN 0-670-83348-7

Produced by Mandarin Offset
Printed and bound in Hong Kong
Set in Bembo

PRAYERS for CHILDREN

~ JULIET · HARMER ~

VIKING

JANUARY

Now the snow is gently falling
and the world is white.
No birds are calling.
Soft flakes drift down
to cover every tree.

We are so lucky to be warm in winter, tucked in
our beds at night. Some people have no homes to
shelter them. We think of them and pray that we
all may be safe and warm.

FEBRUARY

The brave snowdrops push their way
out of the hard earth.
The first lambs are born.
How do they know that Spring
will soon be coming?
How do they know the ground
will soon be warm?

Dear God, let the little lambs be safe, and let the
shepherd find any that are lost in the snow.

MARCH

The wind is cold but the sun is bright.
The stream goes dancing by,
and birds begin to build their nests.
Let us shout and sing and dance
and celebrate the spring.

Thank you for the changing seasons, especially
for the spring that comes each year after the
dark winter.

APRIL

All around me the world is green.
All around me the trees are flowering.
Everything is fresh and new.

Thank you, God, for the brilliant blue of the sky,
for the white dancing clouds, and all the beauty of
the world.

MAY

The wintry weather's truly past,
and children play outside till nearly dark.
Even little dogs join in the fun.

Thank you, God, for making me strong and
healthy. Please take care of all the children who
are ill, and who can't go out to play.

JUNE

I love to be out with my friends
on a summer day
and hear the birds sing high above me.
If only summer could last forever!

Let us always remember to be kind to one
another. If we are loving and caring we shall
always have friends, and if we have friends, we
shall never be sad for long.

JULY

The forest is cool and quiet in the summer,
a place of refuge,
where the animals can rest in the shade.

Thank you, trees, for the shelter you give to birds
and animals, and for the gentle whispering of
your leaves.

AUGUST

If I climbed to the top of that hill,
I could stretch and touch the clouds.
How wonderful to be a cloud and see
the world spread out below.

Please, God, watch over my mother and father
and all my family and friends. Keep them safe
from harm.

SEPTEMBER

The fields of corn are golden.
The fruits and berries are ripening,
ready for the harvest.
Thank you for the sunny mornings
and cool nights of autumn.

Dear God, help us to remember all the children
who do not have enough to eat. Teach us to think
of others before ourselves.

OCTOBER

The sand and the sea and the sky
are all around us.
We hear the sound of the waves
and feel the salt spray on the wind.

We are so lucky to be sheltered and loved. Please
help all the children who have no family to take
care of them. Help me to be generous to others
who have less than I do.

NOVEMBER

Leaves are twirling everywhere –
shaken by the autumn wind,
spinning through the air.

Thank you for time to play and time to work,
time to think and time to dream.

DECEMBER

All the animals are sleeping,
the tree branches are bare.
It's the quietest moment of the year…

Please, God, teach all of your children to live in peace and harmony at home and everywhere in the whole world.